Sit Down, Socks!

Story by
Sally Cowan

Illustrations by
Anne Spudvilas

"Socks," said Rosa.

"This is my doll's stroller.

You can come for a ride in it.

You will like my stroller."

"Sit down, Socks!" said Rosa.

"Please sit down.

 Stay in the stroller!"

"Meow! Meow! Meow!"

"Come back, Socks!" said Rosa.

"Get into the stroller!
We are going for a walk."

"Meow! Meow! Meow!"

Socks ran away.

"Mom," cried Rosa.

"Please help me look for Socks.
He will not stay
in my doll's stroller!"

"I will help you," said Mom.

"Look, Mom!" said Rosa.

"Socks is up in the tree."

"I will get a ladder,"
 said Mom.

Mom went into the garage
to get a ladder.

"Come here, Socks," said Rosa.

Socks came down from the tree, and he ran into the house.

Rosa went inside, too.

"Oh, Socks!" said Rosa.

"You love to sleep on my bed."